All Alone

By
Diane Brookes

Illustrated by
Ann Timmins

Text copyright © 1999 by Diane Brookes
Illustrations copyright © 1999 by Ann Timmins
All rights reserved.
Published by Raven Rock Publishing,
21 Burwash Drive, Yellowknife NT X1A 2V1 CANADA

Canadian Cataloguing in Publication Data

Brookes, Diane.
  All alone

ISBN 0-9683640-9-8

  1. Flowers–Juvenile fiction. I. Timmins, Ann, 1952- II. Title.
PS8553.R6546A84 1999   jC813'.54   C99-910125-0
PZ7.B78979A1 1999

Printed in Yellowknife, Canada, by Artisan Press Ltd.

Dedicated to Sarah O'Donnell,
the flower waiting for her bee!

Once there was a beautiful flower who grew all alone, far from the garden where the other flowers grew. This flower made delicious nectar deep in its throat and grew pollen on its long stamens. Because it was all alone, the beautiful flower needed a friend to carry its pollen to the flowers in the garden.

The beautiful flower stretched out its petals in invitation. Very soon a big fly came by and landed on the outstretched petals. The beautiful flower felt very hopeful.

"May I taste your delicious nectar?" asked the fly.

"You may taste my nectar if you will carry my pollen to the flowers in the garden," answered the flower.

"What? Work for it?" snapped the fly and left in disgust.

Soon an ant walked up
to the beautiful flower.

"May I taste your delicious
nectar?" asked the ant.

"You may taste my nectar
if you will carry my pollen
to the flowers in the
garden," answered the
flower. But the ant only shook
its head and walked away.

Then the beautiful flower felt a tickle on its stem. Looking down it saw a spider climbing up.

"May I taste your delicious nectar?" asked the spider.

"You may taste my nectar if you will carry my pollen to the flowers in the garden," answered the flower.

The spider sighed and dropped back to the ground on a string of silk.

Suddenly the flower felt a brisk breeze; a bright blue dragonfly hovered above it.

"May I taste your delicious nectar?" asked the dragonfly.

"You may taste my nectar if you will carry my pollen to the flowers in the garden," answered the flower.

The dragonfly flew away without a backward glance.

The beautiful flower felt very disappointed. All the bugs wanted to taste the nectar, but none would help take the pollen to the flowers in the garden.

Just then a fumbling, tumbling
bumblebee landed with a tired
plop on the disappointed
flower's drooping petals.

"May I please have some of your
delicious nectar?" asked the
bumblebee, "I'm so tired and
thirsty."

The flower sighed and answered
once more, "You may taste my
nectar if you will carry my pollen
to the flowers in the garden."

"I would be honoured to help you," said the bumblebee with a fat little bow. "Indeed," the bee continued, "my whole life is spent on just such tasks. I carry pollen from one flower to another all day long. That is why I get so very tired."

"Oh, thank you, thank you," said the flower. "I am so grateful to you. Please drink all the nectar you want."

With another funny bow, the bumblebee drank its fill of nectar, filled its baskets with pollen and flew fumbling and tumbling back to the flowers in the garden.

From that day to this, the bumblebee and the beautiful flower have been friends. The bumblebee carries pollen back and forth and the flower keeps making its delicious nectar for the bee's refreshment.

The End.